While I Am Little

While I Am Little

HEIDI GOENNEL

Tambourine Books

New York

To my father

While I am little I can
sleep with my Penguin
and wise old Teddy,

splash in big, muddy puddles
after it rains,

and be a cowboy all day long.

While I am little I can lick
all the icing in the bowl,

take Fluffie for a ride in my wagon,

and collect pennies and stamps
and lots of string.

While I am little I can help
Daddy build a treehouse
in our backyard,

play with my best friend, Pete,

and read under the covers
way into the night.

While I am little I can make a snowman even taller than I am,

go fishing for the whole afternoon,

and see *The Blue-Toed Monster* three times in a row.

And while I am little
I can keep growing up.

Library of Congress Cataloging in Publication Data

Goennel, Heidi. While I am little/by Heidi Goennel.—1st ed. p. cm.
Summary: A child describes splashing in puddles, collecting
things, reading under the covers, building snowmen, and other good
things about being young. [1. Growth—Fiction.] I. Title.
PZ7.G554Wi 1993 [E]—dc20 92-36795 CIP AC
ISBN 0-688-12371-6. —ISBN 0-688-12372-4 (lib. bdg.)
1 3 5 7 9 10 8 6 4 2
First edition

S

94
X

FREE LIBRARY OF
SPRINGFIELD TOWNSHIP
1600 Paper Mill Road
Wyndmoor, Penna. 19118
836-5300

DEMCO